WAGONS WEST!

ROY GERRARD

FARRAR, STRAUS AND GIROUX
NEW YORK

Way back in eighteen-fifty, when Americans were thrifty,
    The times were hard, so most folks had to toil;
My mama, my pa, and me labored hard to guarantee
    That we'd earn a living from the barren soil.

But our lives changed when a man by the name of Buckskin Dan
    Moseyed by and stopped to pass the time of day,
For our entertaining guest had seen rich green land out West—
    Back in Oregon, two thousand miles away.

My enthusiastic pa gathered folks from near and far
    To attend a public meeting in our barn.
When ole Dan described the West, all our neighbors were impressed—
    They could tell it wasn't just an idle yarn.

The idea of Oregon so appealed to everyone
    That without a hitch we made the perfect plan:
We would form a wagon train, and were lucky to retain
    As our trusty guide and leader Buckskin Dan.

So our hopeful little band sold their farmsteads and their land,
    And bought all the things they'd need for that long ride.
We had only slender means, so we stocked up high on beans
    And some other wholesome vittles that were dried.

When our packing was complete, we agreed that we'd all meet
    Up in Independence Town to start our trip.
As we made our rendezvous, some of us were scared, it's true,
    Yet were comforted by our companionship.

The land stretched on forever, but Buckskin Dan was clever
    And his navigation never got us lost,
So we sure were glad of Dan, for we needed such a man
    When six hundred miles of prairie must be crossed.

Then we lurched across the plains through the biting wind and rains,
    Or at times beneath a searing, scorching sun,
And from dawn to dusk each day, as we struggled on our way,
    We all wondered when our journey would be done.

When confronted by a river that made strong men gasp and shiver,
  Dan soon showed us how to reach the other side;
His technique was sure and sound because nobody was drowned,
  And we learned to take such crossings in our stride.

In the evenings before bed, I sat down with Cousin Jed
  As he kindly taught me how to read and write,
For someday I'd pen our tale of adventures on the trail,
  Which I wrote down in my diary every night.

Now and then when things seemed dire, we would sit around the fire,
  While Dan told us of his feats with wolves and bears,
And though everybody knew that his tales weren't always true,
  Well, they helped us to forget our many cares.

With our food stocks running low, Pa dispatched a buffalo,
  Which provided us with meat to eat our fill;
And a short while after that, as we crossed the river Platte,
  We perceived Fort Laramie upon the hill.

There were Pawnees and Shoshones who had come to trade their ponies,
   There were little groups of Flatheads and Cheyenne,
There were Blackfeet, Sioux, and Crow and a few Arapaho,
   And a host of long-time friends of Buckskin Dan.

So we bought provisions here and repaired our broken gear,
   While our mules and cattle had a well-earned rest.
As our journey had been taxing, we needed some relaxing,
   And the dancing was the thing that I liked best.

On the trail again the land turned to sagebrush, rock, and sand,
  Where the waterholes were either fouled or dry.
Every throat was clogged with dust and we knew we simply must
  Find some drinking water soon, or we would die.

Folks began to get downhearted and to wish they'd never started
  On this death-defying, crazy wagon ride,
So it was a pleasant shock to reach Independence Rock
  And the cool Sweetwater River, clear and wide.

While the rest of them recovered, Cousin Jed and I discovered
   A bewildered, frightened, lost Arapaho.
It appeared that Little Thunder (that's the name that he went under)
   Had mislaid his tribe and had nowhere to go.

Not one of us protested when Buckskin Dan suggested
   We should temporarily adopt the child.
Soon, we knew, his friends would find that they'd left the boy behind,
   But till then we couldn't leave him in the wild.

Then some fierce Arapaho, with their leader Mountain Snow,
    Came to ask us if we'd seen their Chieftain's son.
So is it any wonder, when we showed them Little Thunder,
    That their friendship was immediately won?

Reunited with his boy, Mountain Snow was filled with joy—
    He had thought his only son forever lost.
When he heard where we were going, he insisted upon showing
    Where the Rocky Mountains might be safely crossed.

Then we said farewell and parted, but we hardly had restarted
    On our journey when our convoy was attacked.
The bandits, dressed for battle, were out to steal our cattle,
    And our party was too startled to react.

There were bushes all around me and the villains hadn't found me,
    So I galloped off to the Arapaho.
They'd been happy to befriend us and I knew they would defend us,
    When I reached their camp and told my tale of woe.

My description took some time, for I did it all in mime,
    But then Mountain Snow was quick to understand.
He grasped the situation, expressed his indignation,
    And a daring rescue bid was quickly planned.

Well, those varmints weren't too smart and they pretty soon lost heart,
    When our cunning ambush caught them in South Pass.
They could scarce believe their eyes when we took them by surprise,
    After stealthily approaching through the grass.

Then the robbers begged for mercy and their leader, Big Nose Percy,
    Was so frightened that I couldn't help but smile.
A triumphant Mountain Snow then set off, with thieves in tow,
    To Fort Laramie, where they would go on trial.

With the mountains ever steeper and the canyons ever deeper,
    The rocky trail became extremely rough.
We pushed onward, heaving, straining, and though no one was complaining,
    It was obvious that folks had had enough.

After weeks of perspiration, we were close to desperation
    When we reached Columbia River's rocky shore,
Where our prospects looked so slim and the way ahead so grim
    That we felt we could not go on anymore.

For a single day we rested and then Buckskin Dan suggested
    That we build some rafts to float the final lap,
Saying it could spell salvation, even though our destination
    Was still many miles downriver, by the map.

Now in Oregon at last, with all hazards safely past,
    We were thrilled to find a fertile land of dreams.
We settled in Willamette, and I don't think on this planet
    We had ever seen such handsome fields and streams.

Having reached our journey's end I'd be fibbing to pretend
    I'd enjoyed the dangers that we'd had to share.
Yet the truth that I had learned was that triumph must be earned,
    And that fortune often smiles on those who dare.

As I sit and write today, twenty years have rolled away,
    And the fair Willamette's still our happy home,
Where the corn is growing high underneath a cloudless sky—
    It's the place from which we never wish to roam.

Copyright © Roy Gerrard 1996
All rights reserved
First published in Great Britain by Victor Gollancz, 1996
Printed in Singapore by Imago
First American edition, 1996
Second printing, 1996

Library of Congress Cataloging-in-Publication Data
Gerrard, Roy.
Wagons West!/Roy Gerrard.—1st American ed.
[1. Overland journeys to the Pacific—Fiction. 2. Frontier and
pioneer life—Fiction. 3. Stories in rhyme.] I. Title.
PZ8.3.G323Wag 1996 [E]—dc20 95-276 CIP AC